# Dedication

This book is dedicated to all those who've experienced hurt by a narcissistic partner in their lifetime. We reside in A world where most people disguise their struggles instead of seeking assistance to cease the cycle. Most are unaware that there is a cycle. Love is ultimately the cure for a peaceful world. In order to love, you must be at peace within yourself to completely understand someone else. Until a person finds themselves and learns how to properly love, they will destroy everything they're in contact with.

Thank you to everyone that contributed to my personal life lessons. Most importantly I'd like to thank God himself for keeping me when I was a lost man, shattering hearts. Loving one woman, trumps trying to have intercourse with multiple strangers any day of the week.

## Table Of Content

1. Man Of Her Dreams
2. Alisha's Way or The Highway
3. Steven's Thoughts
4. Suspicious Acts
5. Rachel's Life
6. Alisha Always Gets Her Way, Every Time
7. Trouble
8. Why Steven
9. Lost It All
10. Temptation
11. What's Wrong
12. Blast From The Past
13. J
14. Deceit
15. Love Lost
16. Regret
17. Zena Meets Rachel
18. Until A Man Finds Himself, He Will Destroy Everything He Touches
19. What Did You Do
20. What To Do
21. Do You Trust Me
22. Lady's Night

### ***Triangle of love***

# Chapter 1

*Man of her Dreams*

  Steven Washington comes home from work; he sees his beautiful Four-month pregnant girlfriend Zena Meyer. She was laying on the couch exhausted from the long day she as well. Steven walks over to the couch to give Zena a kiss her on her forehead, that when he noticed she's wearing his favorite color lingerie that he suggested she should wear the night they made passionate love and created their bundle of joy. They both didn't want to know the sex of the baby until He or She was born. Steven began to kiss on her neck as she wakes up playing as if she wants him to stop. She reached in for a hug as they continued to greet each other with love. He takes off his blazer, loosened his tie and unbutton his work shirt. Revealing his chisel chest and rock solid 6 pack, Zena felt herself starting to get moist. Steven looks down and noticed the juices from her pussy lips soaking up the couch. He takes his shirt off and puts his long black and brown dreadlocks in a ponytail. He lifts her legs to pick her up and put them around his head. He proceeded to lick and suck every drop of her juices that fell from her swollen clit. Zena's throbbing clit could only take a few licks from Steven's tongue, before she began to cum so hard that her body shook. He continued to suck away at her womanhood. He placed her down gently on the Alpaca Carpet and slid her lingerie to the side. He unzipped his pants, Zena's mouth begun to water as she stares eye to eye with his already rock hard ten-inch penis. Steven then palms his own manhood and strokes it a few times before he tries to enter Zena's throbbing love canal. She stops him and tells him to "lay back." so she can give him oral pleasure. She pushed him back onto the couch with slight force. Zena began to suck and slob all over Steven's dick.

    He started to tell her how his day went but couldn't form the words to say because of how Zena was stroking his manhood and slurping his balls all in one motion. Steven stops her before he released. He positioned her on her back and started to rub her clit with the tip of his penis as she begs for him to put it inside her. The anticipation was overwhelming but a must, he begun to slide into her with a stroke that made her gasp for air, Zena let out a sexy moan and whispered into his ear "This yo pussy daddy, I love you, go deeper." Steven continued to take her to ecstasy with long deep strokes as he played with her nipples and kissed softly on the neck. He asked her "Am I too deep?", he said joking "I don't want my dick hitting the baby." They both started laughing. He gets off Zena and tells her to turn around. She assumes the doggy style position and he licks her pussy from the back. She begins to moan heavily, he gave her deeper strokes and grabbed her waist, pulling her back into his pelvis. Steven took control of her pussy like he owned it. As she moaned and screamed for more, he looked down at his phone that had slightly fallen out of his pants pocket and saw he had an incoming call. He looks at the screen and noticed the name *"Alisha"* pops up. He leans to the side while stroking Zena's pussy and declined the call. Zena felt him move. She looked back at him and asked, "What are you doing?" he replied, "Nothing baby, just a call from the office, I'll call them back later." He continued to thrust away at Zena's swollen pussy lips,  She screams out "cum daddy" "cum for me." He smacks her round booty and watched it jiggle while he hit it from behind. Steven tells her he's about to cum and ask her "where do you want me to put it?" she replied, "Wherever you want, I'm all yours." He grunts and moan while releasing his semen into her wet box.

  He kissed her on the forehead, grabs his shirt and pants then headed to the bedroom to take a shower. Zena laid on the carpet body still shaking from the amazing strokes he laid upon her.

    Steven entered the master bedroom and grabbed a towel, while looking down at his phone reading the messages Alisha Banks texted him. *"I know you with her, so don't call me until you're out of love with her." "I hate that you always go home to her."* He shakes his head and turns on the hot water. He sits on the tub debating should he text or call her back. In the mist of him responding to Alisha's messages, he receives a call from her again. "Hello!!!" he says, Alisha then began to cry about how she misses him and needs him to come over. He responds and tell her "Look!!, I'm just getting in, give me a few hours, I'll come by." He hangs up as Zena walks in overhearing the conversation and saying, "Hell No!! Not tonight, no hanging with the guys, no overtime at work, just me you and the baby." He smiles, gets in the shower and tells her "Baby, we have a big case we're working on at the moment. We need all the pieces to connect in order for everything to go right. I have to go, but I promise I won't be long."  He continues to wash his body while she stares at the soap running from his chest to his dick, she always admired his brown beautiful skin. While in a daze, Zena says "only if I could get another round," he turns around and tells her to get in.  Steven bends her over and she places her hands against the wall. He starts to kiss her neck, while spreading her legs, she stands on her tippy toes and leaned forward as he slides his dick inside her. He rubs her nipples while he strokes her pussy in and out. They both climaxed an enormous amount of times. Zena and Steven laid in bed and talked, as she laid on his chest playing in his dreads, she asked him "Are you happy with me?" "Yes love, I am why you ask that?" he replied, "I'm just wondering babe, everything seems so surreal at times. Thanks for being the man of my dreams." She gloated. Steven then kissed Zena on the forehead and whispered in her ear

"Your definitely welcome." They both were exhausted and fell fast asleep.

 The next day Steven woke up to *15 missed calls* and *10 text messages* from Alisha. He began to read the messages, when he heard "Good morning handsome." Zena walks in with breakfast draped in her silk red Robe, she greets him with a kiss as he slides his phone under the pillow. "Thank you, babe!" he replied, as he took his hand to move a piece of her hair that got in the way of their kiss. Zena kissed him back and went into the closet to get dressed for work. While they were eating breakfast

Steven's phone started to ring again. He declined the call smoothly. Steven then moved the breakfast trey from in front of him to signal he was done and rushed to get dressed. Zena came out of the closet puzzled as to why Steven was moving so fast getting dressed. "Are you in a rush love?" She speaks. "Yes I have to hurry and get to the office, the meeting has already started," he replies. Zena chuckles at him because he was moving so fast, he put his shoes on the wrong feet and didn't realize it until he started to walk. "See you later Daffy Duck." Zena says to him as he rushes out the door. She closed the front door and walked back towards the bedroom. Zena stops in the living room to pick up her clothes that laid on the floor, from the previous night of intimacy. She picked up his shirt. Zena took a whiff of it to smell his scent, she's somewhat obsessed with the man of her dreams, and she loves the way he smells. She noticed it has a woman's perfume stench to it. Her pregnancy senses were heighted, so every scent was very noticeable. Zena formed a frown on her face as she walks back to the bedroom to get dressed.

# Chapter 2
*"Alisha's way or the highway"*

While lying in her queen size bed with satin Sheets laying across her naked body Alisha continues to call Steven on the phone. Steven finally picks up, He tries to sweet talk her, but she cuts him off mid-sentence. "Get here now." She hangs the phone up and throws it across her bedroom. Alisha laid back down and waits for Steven to arrive. While on his way to Alisha, he got a call from Zena. He denied the call and texts her back saying," I'm in a meeting I'll call you back." He pulls into

Alisha's driveway.  He got out the car, walked up the driveway and stopped to admire the new Mercedes Benz. He bought it a few days ago for her birthday.
Steven continued to walk to Alisha's front door inserting his key. He walked through Alisha's house up to her bedroom. He finds her

laying naked in her bed sleeping peacefully after all her crazy calls and threatening text messages. Steven began to grab his manhood as it became rock hard while he walked closer and notice her coke bottle shaped body wrapped in red satin sheets. He grew closer and kissed her on the lips. She woke up surprised and pushed him off her. Alisha began to question him about why he didn't come over the previous night. Steven replies "I had a long day yesterday at the office. I took a hot shower and went to sleep," he said as he snuck a kiss on her neck and continued to her lips. Alisha couldn't resist, she kissed him back and laid back as he kissed on her neck and then towards her nipples. Alisha pushed the covers back and said, "come eat this pussy, don't tell me your sorry show me." Steven loved the way Alisha's pussy taste, so the command made him smile. He lifted her legs onto his broad shoulders and began to kiss and suck Alisha's clit. Alisha squirms across the satin sheets, with a hand full of Steven locs. He continued to devour her pussy, she moans louder and louder as she begins to cum her legs shaking uncontrollably. Steven takes off his Armani blazer and pants and laid on top of Alisha. He questioned her "Are you ready for daddy dick?" she replied back "fuck this pussy like it's your last time." Steven inserted his dick inside of Alisha's warm tight pussy, she gasps from the first stroke and asked her "Well is it my last time?" she screams out "NO DADDY, this your pussy forever, I love you." He continued to give her long thrusting hard strokes. During their erotic session, Steven's phone rings again. But this time it's a call from his boss. He reaches over to look at his phone, Alisha says "call whoever that is back,

I was just about to cum again." Steven gets up to take the call, leaving Alisha upset laying in the bed. After his phone call he told Alisha he had to leave, they need him at the office. Alisha sat on the bed upset with her arms folded and lips poked out, as if she was a child upset about not getting any candy. It didn't bother Steven because one thing about him his work always came before pleasure. He walked in the bathroom and turned the shower on to wash off the scent of sex before going to the office and home later. Alisha tried to get in the shower with him, "You have to wait Alisha I really have to go." Alisha didn't take too kindly to the brush off. She left the bathroom and got dressed swiftly, she ran downstairs and grabbed a knife. She went towards the front door and down the driveway to where Steven parked his Bentley. She slashed one of his tires so he couldn't leave. She rushed back in the house and into the kitchen while Steven was getting dressed. He makes his way into the kitchen, Alisha was acting as if she was about to start making breakfast, grabbing things out of the fridge. Steven askes her "Is everything alright?" she replies back "mmhh huh, everything is just fine, you hungry?"

"No thank you, I should be going" as he grabbed his keys and walked out the door. Alisha smiled with a devilish grin knowing he would be back. Steven walked down the walkway and gets into his car headed to work. He starts to reverse down the driveway when he noticed his tire sensor on his car came on. He pulls over and gets out, walks around looking at his tires and notices his rear passenger tire is flat. He couldn't tell that it was slashed due to him riding on the tire and the rim started to come out of it. Steven starts cursing profusely because he knows he's going to be late for one of the most important meetings of his career. His boss asked him to be at the meeting with a stellar presentation for their new client. Alisha looks out the window waiting for Steven to pull back up any minute now but instead her phone rings. It's a call from Steven now she's nervous that he may have noticed the slash in his tire, so she preps herself before answering. She picks up; Steven says "Hey I caught a flat tire and the tow company is 30 minutes away." Alisha gets upset and ends the call without saying goodbye. She slammed the phone on the countertop and began to shake her head and talking to herself, mad that her plan didn't go as she thought it would. Steven calls his boss and lets him know he would not be able to make it in time for the meeting. His boss didn't take it well and told him to take the rest of the day off and try again tomorrow.

Steven hits his steering wheel cussing so loud the car next to him could hear it.

Chapter 3
*"Steven's Thoughts"*

As the tow company repairs the slash tire with a spare. Steven stands aside thinking to himself what a day it had been already. He decided to go to a nearby bar for a drink to ease his mind. Steven walked in a local bar during happy hour, the drinks are always half off which brought a lot of people to the venue. It was filled with cigarette smoke and happy people dancing to old tunes. Steven walked up to the bar and orders

2 shots of Louis Xlll. He loosens up his necktie and began to take his first shot. He threw it back and held his chest as the Remy began to burn as it went down his throat. He took a deep breath and began to think to himself: *"Man, this shit is becoming a handful. I got to get it together,*

*missing out on money man, I'm tripping, I'm letting pussy get to me I got a baby on the way. Fuck Man, I gotta leave Alisha alone."*

Steven takes another shot, then signals for the waitress to bring him a Long Island, and 2 more shots of Louie XIII. Steven takes the other shot and sips his Long

Island as he began to think again.

"I think, I'm in love with them both but is that even possible. Shitttt, this love thing is so stressful. Maybe I should just be single, and a bachelor.

Nah, cause I don't want my kid growing up thinking it's ok to play *with hearts."*

Steven takes his last shot. *"Maybe I should just tell Alisha the truth, I can't leave my family."*

Steven takes another sip of his Long Island looking at all the happy couples dancing to *"If this world were mine" by Luther Vandross*

He begins to think of all the good times he and

Zena had. Deep down inside he knows Zena has his heart, but his lust for Alisha is uncontrollable. Steven continues to drink his Long Island. Then this beautiful medium height woman with black long curly hair, dressed in a silky top with black pants, and red bottom heels caught his eye. She sat at the bar pulling out a stool next to his and ordered a martini. Steven couldn't help but notice her sweet smelling aroma, it drew him to her instantly. He smelled it over the Cigarette smoke.

He acknowledged her and let her know how good she smelled, starting a friendly conversation. She looked exhausted from her day. "Looks like you had a long day." he said "Yeah, I had a long day, I have so many clients that their problems are starting to take a toll on me. One of my long-term clients didn't take my advice. I just found out she took her own life after finding out her husband was cheating on her." She replied

"I'm sorry to hear that, my day is going, it could be better. I had a flat tire and I missed one of the biggest meetings in my life. Not only that my boss told me to take the day off. I hate missing money. Sounds like I need a therapist."

Steven laughed "Well you just met one." she replied. The two continues to converse about life and everything going on in their lives. They ordered more drinks as, Steven looked down at his Rolex, time had flown by. Great conversation and shots of Louie will do that to you. Steven says to her,

"I should be going, I have to get up early. I don't want to miss work tomorrow; I probably won't have a job." they both laughed. "I'm sorry I didn't catch your name?" steven chuckled "How rude of me." "It's ok honey, I didn't catch yours either." she said playfully "I'm Rachel Whitmoore." "It's nice to meet you Rachel I'm Steven Washington, you can just call me Steve. Can I call you sometime, maybe have another friendly date?"

"Another?" She playfully replies, "Who said this was a date?" She smacked her lips "I'm just kidding, here's my card give me a call any time after 4pm or before

10am, that's when I start my sessions." Steven takes her card and gives her a friendly hug before leaving. "You want me to walk you to your car?" he asked respectfully. "That's ok I'm gonna have another drink before leaving." She smiled devilishly. Steven winks at her and walks out the bar.

"Damnit Steve, here you go again
Man, you have a too much going on as it is."

"But damn she was an angel right out of heaven, Fuck, maybe I should just throw this card out, I don't need no more pussy in my life."

*Steven's phone rings: Zena.*

Steven answered, "Hey baby, I'm just leaving the office, I'll be home soon." "Ok Steven" she replies.

From the "Ok Steven" he could feel she was upset about something. Steven put Rachel's card in his wallet and drove off to see what was wrong with

Zena. As he heads home, he continues to think of a way he can cut Alisha off and to his surprise she starts calling him.

*Ring: Alisha*

He denied the phone call because he was not far from home. Alisha texted him saying *"call me it's urgent."* Steven pulled over to call before arriving home.

 Alisha picks the phone up screaming. "It's in here, come help me!" "What's wrong?" he shouted. "Just get here Steven hurry up before it gets me." Alisha replied. Steven hangs the phone up and turns around just a block from his home and heads towards Alisha. When Steven arrived at Alisha's house he ran up to the door and opened it with his key. Alisha heard him come in, "Come upstairs, hurry." She said frantically. Steven ran upstairs with his .40 cal Glock in hand ready for whatever. He slowly opens the door to her bedroom and Alisha is standing on her bed panicking over a spider on the wall. Steven yells "This is what you called me here for, what the fuck Alisha. I'm thinking it's something serious it's just a spider." "Glad to see you'd come to my rescue, now kill it." she says to him. Steven kills the spider and walks towards the bedroom door. "Is that all you wanted?" "No, I wanted you to come put this pussy to sleep." she says. "No, Alisha I have to go, I'll see you tomorrow." Steven said sternly, as he walks out the bedroom and downstairs to the front door. He slams the door as he walks to his car. He gets in the car and begins to think:

*"This Shit gotta stop."* as he drove off, headed home.

## Chapter 4
*Suspicious acts*

Zena sat in the living room on the love seat, patiently waiting for

Steven's arrival. She began to think to herself; *"Maybe I'm tripping, Steven would never cheat on me, I'm carrying his child for Christ's sake. But I've never smelled that scent before."* As Zena thinks to herself, she sees his headlights reflect in the window from the front room. "Steven's home."

As Steven pulls into the driveway, he sits inside his car getting his mind together, he didn't want to seem irritated about Alisha's spider call. Steven also remembers Zena called him by his first name, which signified to him that she was upset about something. Steven exited his vehicle and began to walk toward the house. When Steven walked in and to his surprise, he saw Zena on the love seat sitting in her Versace robe with her arms folded across her chest. "I have something I wanna ask you before the rest of this evening continues on." she cut straight to the point. Steven could tell she was suspicious or something, so he replied "Well, hey to you as well, my love." "Hello, Steven." She cut. "I was cleaning up and I picked your shirt up and noticed it had a women's scent on it." Steven grabs his head and replies, "Zena are you serious right now, I had 3 clients yesterday and 2 were women maybe one of their perfume scents got on me as I greeted them with a hug and handshake." Zena thinks to herself; *Damn maybe I am tripping.* "I'm sorry baby it's this pregnancy, I can smell everything. I noticed another woman scent on you and lost it." she cried. Steven was in disbelief, he didn't think she would believe him so easily, he thought for sure Zena knew about Alisha. He replied "It's ok baby I get it, I'd trip too if I smelled another man's cologne on you. I'm about to shower I had a long day at the office." Zena then frowns and asks him another question, "Baby what time did you get in the office? I called your phone and didn't get an answer. I talked to your boss, and he told me he sent you home." Steven stopped midway up the stairwell and lifted his head up shaking it. He replied "Yeah, he sent me home, so I went out for a drink and saw an old client there. We had a few drinks and now I'm here honey love."  Zena said to herself: *Ok, yeah I'm really tripping now.* "I'm sorry baby, it won't happen again, I don't know what I was thinking." Zena replied. Steven continued up the stairs to the bedroom to take his shower. Zena sits back on the love seat and has a conversation with herself, *"Yeah I won't do that again. I don't wanna run him away being crazy, get it together Zena."* She walks up the stairs and heads for the bedroom. After Steven showered, he laid in the bed next to Zena cuddling up under her and her baby bump, as if he was a little child looking for their mother's warm body. Zena runs her fingers through his locs as he falls sound asleep in her arms. Zena couldn't sleep, something was bothering her the whole night. She got out of the bed and began to pace the floor silently while Steven slept. Thinking to herself: *What is bothering me I just can't figure it out, is my Woman's intuition kicking in? Fuck!* As she paced back and forth, she trips over Steven's pants that he left on the floor while getting in the shower. Zena picked the pants up and Steven's wallet fell onto the floor. She picks it up and a card is sticking out of it as if it was recently placed in there. Steven wakes up reaching for Zena and realizes she is not in the bed. He sits up and Zena drops the card and wallet before getting a chance to read it. "What are you doing baby?" he asks "I'm going to the bathroom; the baby is pushing down on my bladder." she walks towards the bathroom in the master bedroom. Zena goes into the bathroom and closes the door, she paces back and forth shaking her hands, thinking to herself: *"Shit that was close, Zena what has gotten into you. Get your shit together, are going through his wallet now, what the fuck?"* Zena flushed the toilet as if she was using the bathroom and turns the water on to wash her hands to make them wet. She opens the door and is startled by Steven standing there. "Is Everything ok love? I'm just making sure you and my baby are ok." "Yeah, were fine, baby" Zena replied coyly. "Come back to bed, so I can hold you," Steven grabbed Zena by the hand and led her to the bed. As he walked back, he noticed his wallet laying on the ground and Rachel's card sticking out of it. "Baby I'm about to get some water you want some?" "No thank you," Zena says unenthusiastically. Steven let go of Zena's hand as she got in the bed and walked toward the bedroom door. On his way out he picked up his pants and his wallet and tucked the card deeper inside so that it wouldn't be visible. Steven sat his pants inside his dirty clothes hamper and his wallet on the dresser and walked out of the bedroom to get some water. On his way downstairs Steven

thought to himself: *"Man I wonder if she saw that shit? It's just a therapist card, nothing wrong with that, right.*
*I should've just thrown that damn card out man, Alisha's ass through me off."*

Steven drinks some water and heads backs

upstairs. Zena laid in the bed waiting for Steven to come back in the room. She had slipped on a pink thong that complemented Her dark skin and curvy body, knowing Steven couldn't resist the way she looked in it. He walked in the bedroom and saw Zena with her ass up face down in doggy style position waiting for him to come tame what's was his. "Damn that's how you feel?" Steven walks up to the bed and slides Zena's pink thong to the side and begin to eat her pussy and suck on her clit. He licks and fingers her ass sending goosebumps down Zena spine and plays with her clit while doing so. Zena screams out "I'm ready daddy, fuck me." Steven flips Zena over and slides his dick inside of her, giving her slow strokes just the way, she likes it. All the while Steven is fucking Zena he is thinking about Alisha, Zena notices his facial expressions, and ask "Is everything ok, baby?"

"Yes" he replied as he continues to stroke her pussy, he pulls his dick out, and tells Zena to turn around, she told him to wait, she wanted to get something off her mind, and began to give him oral pleasure. While pleasing steven with her mouth, Steven thought to himself, *"Damn Alisha don't suck dick like this, fuck."* He tells her he's about to Cum and asks "Where do you want it?" she replies, "In my Mouth." as he closed his eyes and lifted his head back onto the headboard, holding Zena hair out of the way so it doesn't get wet. He screams out "ahhh shit I love you baby fuck," as he cums uncontrollably inside of her mouth. They both laughed as the intense Moment had come to an end. Forgetting all about the thoughts of infidelity beforehand. They went to sleep peacefully holding each other.

Chapter 5
*Rachel's Life*

Rachel's day was coming to an end with her last client. All she could think about was when the next time she would see Steven. Rachel admired his handsome smile, and great conversation, most of all she loved the way he carried himself. "How does Monday next week sound for your next session?" she asked the heartbroken woman who sat on the plush black leather couch crying her eyes out. She had recently found out about her husband's affair. "Yes, that's fine Rach" she replied, sobbing and crying continuously. Rachel sat in her chair with her legs folded, and her notepad in her hands feeling sorry for her client. She sat everything down, and went to give her a hug, trying to comfort her broken heart. The woman hugged her back and asked; "Rachel are you single?" "Yes, why'd you ask?"

"Stay that way", she replied as she loosened up her hug from Rachel. "I'll be sure to keep that in mind honey, see you next week" Rachel said, as the woman exited Rachel's office. Rachel sat at her office desk and went in a daze thinking of how her love life would be.

*"I wonder if my husband would do me the way my clients did her.*

*Sometimes it is their fight, I just don't know how to tell them, and not sound like a rude bitch."*

Rachel's thought's get interrupted from a call on her office phone, she fumbles to answer due to the daze she was in. "Hel.. hello, Rachel speaking how can I help you?" A deep familiar voice is on the other end of the phone, that Rachel recognizes, but isn't quite sure who it is.

"Hey, love its Steven, I'm on break at work and was thinking of you, so I decided to give you a ring." Rachel snapped back into reality fast, "Hey Handsome, how are you? I just wrapped up with my last client for the day." Steven and Rachel continue to conversate for the duration of his lunch break. "Hey I should be getting back in the office now, let's do drinks over at Lilies, about 7:30 pm?"

"Sure" Rachel replied as she blushed like a schoolgirl. "Great see you then." The two hung up their phones, thinking of seeing one another later. Rachel leaned back in her chair and did her happy dance as a sign of relief, he finally called her after 3 days. Rachel gathered all her paperwork and her belongings and jetted out the door.  She wanted to get home and freshen up before her date this evening. Rachel arrived home, to her surprise her ex-boyfriend had left flowers on her doorstep with a note that quoted *"I'm sorry, please take me back."* She smelled the flowers and walked toward the dumpster and threw them away. She walked away smiling and headed for her mini mansion.

Rachel looked in her closet pulling numerous dresses out. Placing them against her body and throwing them on the bed to see which one would fit the best and shows off her curves. She finds the perfect fit, a black dress with the word Burberry at the bottom trim in brown letters. She grabbed her

Burberry heels, and purse to match. She laid her dress on the bed, and heads toward the bathroom to take a shower dancing and singing "Twerkulator" by The City Girls.

 Chapter 6

*"Alisha Always gets her way, every time"*

Alisha went for a drive, and decided to go to Somerset mall, for some retail therapy. As she walked in the mall all the guys turned their heads as if they were in the movie The Exorcise. She wore skintight jeans that showed her big booty, her red bottom heels complemented her walk as they clicked on the ground. She switched her hips side to side walking towards the skywalk headed to the more expensive side of the mall. Alisha owned her own boutique, and a hair salon downtown. Fashion and keeping her hair done was always a priority on her list. She walked in the Gucci store and gathered everything she wanted; her balance came to a total of $6,500. Alisha reached in her purse and grabbed her wallet to pay the cashier. She opened the wallet and went for her credit card. She noticed she still has one of Steven's cards, from her birthday when he told her to go on a shopping spree with a max of

"$10,000". She grabs his card to make the purchase. "Thank you!" the cashier said after handing Alisha her bags with her new Gucci purse and heels to match. Alisha headed to the Louis Vuitton store next. She noticed a matching set of LV shoes for men and women. She thought to herself *"It's his money, I guess I can get him something."* as she walked into the store waving for a cashier to come to her. Right after her purchase she gets a phone call from Steven "What the hell are you doing Alisha?" "ahh, just a little retail therapy, on you, seeing how I can't get some time, and happiness from you I figured some gifts will do." She said in a sassy tone. Steven sighed over the phone. "Look Alisha, I'll see you tomorrow this is getting out of hand now." Alisha didn't care what Steven was talking about as she continued walking through the mall headed towards the Victoria's Secret, for their new spring collection. "I'm getting bad reception honey. I'll see you tomorrow and you will be staying the night, right Steven?" "Ok, Alisha," he replied before hanging up. She smirked as she walked into the store and said out loud to herself "Alisha always gets her way, every time" and headed toward the lingerie section.

## Chapter 7

*Trouble*

Rachel arrived at the restaurant, and was greeted by the hostess, a beautiful dark skin woman with a soft voice. "How can I help you be beautiful?" She asked Rachel. Wait let me guess you're here for Mr. Steven?" "Yes", Rachel replied blushing. "Right this way." She said pointing in steven's direction. Steven sat at the intimate round table with white cloth seats, a small candle lit between the two seats. He sipped his shot of don Julio as he awaited Rachel's arrival. As she got closer all she could do was smile, so did Steven as he stood to pull out her chair, greeting her with flowers and a hug. "Thank you, Steve, you smell so good, what do you have on?" she asked "Creed." He replied blushing, "You look so beautiful, I think I need to set some appointments up so I can see you more." Rachel continued to smile and joke back with Steven. The night was going great, until Steven's phone started to go off. "You can answer that, I don't mind," Rachel said. "Oh, it's just work, it can wait." The two continued their evening talking about their goals and future, but Steven's mind was all over the place because he was getting calls from Alisha, and his pregnant fiancé Zena. Steven thoughts:

"Man, what does this damn girl want? She wants me to

*prolly come kill another spider or some shit. Swear I need to cut her ass off, Rachel can take her place. Nah I need to chill; I keep forgetting I'm about to get married. I wonder why Zena called. I should at least shoot her a message just to check on her.*
*Nah that a be too rude, imma just go to the bathroom and check on her."*

"Whew, I think I had wayyyy too many shots, excuse me while I run to the restroom real fast." Steven lies as he gets up and takes his phone with him to the restroom.

Rachel's Thoughts:
"This guy is so wonderful.
 I can't wait to show this one off.
He smells so damn Good.
This gotta be too good to be true.

*I wonder why he took his phone with him though, that shit was going off a little too much. He's probably in there responding to their calls. Stop Rachel, you trippin you just met this man. They're not all the same chill."*

Steven walks in the restroom and hides in a stall. He pulled his phone out and began to text Alisha. After texting Alisha, he calls

Zena. "Hey baby, I should be finishing up with this last client soon, do you need anything before I come home?" he lied again. Steven hangs up and walks out the stall to wash his hands, so it seems as if he was really using the restroom. Rachel orders another round of drinks for the two as Steven walks up to the table. "I feel much better now." Steven says to

Rachel. As they continued their conversation and finished their drinks the two began to feel a sensation coming over them. Steven signals for the waitress to bring the bill, he starts to reach in his back pocket to retrieve his wallet, at the same time Rachel digs in her clutch purse and pulls out an American Express Black card. "I got it love" Rachel replied. That made Stevens dick hard because he's always the one paying for things. The fact that she had a Black card let him know the level of woman he's dealing with. He reached inside of his wallet and tipped the waitress $200. He put his suit jacket on and headed towards the exit walking out hand and hand with Rachel. The valet Pulled his Rolls Royce around to the door, as he approached his vehicle, he opened the passenger door and told Rachel to get in. He walked around to the driver side of the car and drove off. Rachel was in a daze because she never rolled in a Rolls Royce. He reached over and grabbed her by the hand and began to kiss her. Steven pulled over into an empty lot, put his car in park and leaned over to give Rachel a kiss as she kissed back. The two crawled into the back seat of the Rolls Royce and began to kiss passionately as if they were both holding it in for the longest. They began to undress themselves, throwing their clothes onto the floor. Rachel laid back while Steven put a condom on that he had stashed in his glove compartment. He lifts her legs up and begins to devour her pussy with his tongue as if it was his last meal. Rachel moans and screams loudly grabbing his locs, grinding her pussy lips against his tongue and beard, as she cums in his mouth. He sits up, wipes her juices off his face and begins to kiss her as he lays on top of her. He put her legs up over his shoulders so he could go deep inside of her tight pussy. Steven could tell her pussy hadn't been touched in a while due to how tight it was and the way her body reacts every time he digs deeper in her guts. Steven's pants were halfway down so he stopped and turned her around to hit it from the back. He took his pants off and began smacking her on her ass and rubbing his dick against her clit before putting his penis inside her. He was so tempted to take the condom off so that he could feel her insides, but he didn't want to risk getting her pregnant, unlike Alisha she couldn't get pregnant. Steven continues to thrust her pussy with long hard strokes, Rachel tries to run, but Steven pulls her back into his pelvis making his shaft go deeper inside of her. The two continued to have wild sex in the back of his $100,000 car, changing positions, not caring if anyone noticed. During the last switch Steven's phone began to vibrate in his pants pocket. He didn't feel it going off because at this point his pants were down around his ankles. Steven sat back while Rachel pulls the condom off and began to suck his dick. Steven moved his leg and his foot stepped on the phone answering the call from Zena by mistake. "Hey baby I figured out what else you can grab from the sto"... Zena hears moaning through the phone mid-sentence, she stops and listens. Steven continues to get his dick sucked by Rachel who is grunting and moaning because she does it so well. He grabs her by the back of her head and shoves his dick deeper in her mouth as he cums.

The two laughs about what just happened while they got

dressed. Steven never noticed his phone was answered. Zena grabs her stomach and begins to start crying and breathing heavily, uncontrollably, she looks down and notices her pants are wet.

Her water broke she was going into shock. She screams on the phone for Steven, but he couldn't hear because he was listening to music and talking with

Rachel on the way back to her car. The two finally arrived at the restaurant where she left her car and she hated that the night was coming to an end. Steven gets out of the car and opens Rachel's door he embraced her with a tight hug and kiss before letting her get in her car to leave. As Steven watches Rachel drive away, he reaches for his phone in his pocket to check the time.  His eyes get wide when he realizes Zena had called and the phone answered. He looked at the call log it showed she was on the phone for 34 minutes.

Steven scrambles to get in his Rolls Royce and burns rubber pulling off so fast trying to get home. On the way home he debated calling Zena back. The guilt was so heavy that he passed a few stop signs and ran a few red lights but didn't notice the Michigan State Trooper that was sitting off to the side clocking his vehicle's speed. Steven looks in his rear-view mirror and the state trooper had his lights on him signaling him to pull over.

Chapter 8
*"Why Steven"*

Zena laid on the stretcher getting wheeled into the Emergency room.

All she could think about was the conversation she just heard Steven having with another woman, not to mention the moaning. The nurses tried to calm her down as they informed her that she's having a miscarriage. "You need to control your breathing because your blood pressure 131 is too high." The lead nurse explained. She began to cry loudly screaming to the top of her lungs because of what the nurse just told her. The nurses finally got her to calm down by sedating her.

Zena wakes up hours later, confused
about what's going on. As she laid there a nurse walks in and announces herself as Nurse Terry. She tells Zena

that she's going to be taking care of her during her stay. Zena asks the nurse "Why am I here, what happened?" "Relax honey." nurse Terry said with a sweet voice. "You came in panicking and your hormone levels were dropping fast. It appears your water broke, I'm so sorry to tell you this but because your water broke so early in your pregnancy your baby did not make it. The baby no longer has a heartbeat. You're going to undergo an emergency procedure, and you will have to be induced so that the fetus can be removed from your uterus. I'm so sorry."

"So, your telling me that my child will be born dead?" Zena began to cry profusely. "This is a nightmare."

The nurse rushed over to soothe her and began to prep her for the procedure, she informed her that the longer she waited the more of a health risk it became for her own mortality. "I'm sorry" the nurse said, "It's not your fault sometimes these things just happen." Zena couldn't respond as tears fell from her eyes, clouding her thoughts and mind. The nurse rushed her to Labor & Delivery where Zena gave birth to their 2lbs baby boy, who died on his birthday. After the procedure Nurse Terry came to check on Zena. "How are you feeling sweetheart?"

"Just give me a moment to myself please." Zena instructed the nurse to leave. As Zena sat back in the hospital bed, she began to remember everything. All she could do was cry and kept asking "why Steven?" in a low voice. She laid in there with her eyes closed thinking

to herself where she could've gone wrong.
She thought to herself:
*"I did everything right"*
*"I thought I was his everything we were even engaged, in Love, why Steven"*
*"I should've known from the unanswered phone calls, texts and late-night working shit was all a lie"*

*"I can't believe I lost my baby because of this shit."*

*"There will be hell to pay, that's on my baby. If he thinks he's about to get away with this, watch this."*

Zena's thoughts were interrupted by the nurse coming in to check her vitals and offering her some food from the menu. "Thank you, but no thank you. I don't really have an appetite right now." Zena replied. "Can I ask you a question, have you ever been cheated on?"

"Yes, the nurse replied I have a few times. That's why I'm single now. I work 16 hours 6 days a week just to keep from getting in a relationship. Most of these guys don't want shit from us. You can do everything right and still get left." Nurse Terry says to Zena. The two continued to have a conversation about their problems and life. At the end of the conversation the nurse offered Zena a number to a therapist who specializes in relationship problems she felt the therapist could assist her with healing. Zena takes down the therapist number and asks, "What's her name?" The nurse says, "her name is Rachel Whitmoor." She tells the nurse thank you and ends up ordering something off the menu. She worked up an appetite after venting about her problems.

Meanwhile Steven is back at home sitting in his driveway contemplating on what to say to Zena, when he knows he has been caught red handed.

Steven finally builds enough courage to walk in the house, but to his surprise she wasn't there. He walked in the kitchen, the bathrooms, checked the basement and the master and guest bedroom. He began to get frustrated because he couldn't find her, yelling through the house going room to room with no response.  Steven decided to give her a call for the first time. As he called her phone, he heard something going off in the kitchen he went to see what the noise was. It was Zena's phone on the marble countertop buzzing from Steven's call. At that point Steven felt as if everything was over. She'd found out about Rachel and left him for good with no way for him to contact her.

 Steven began to panic, throwing things around the house.

Chapter 9

## "Lost It All"

As days went on Steven hadn't heard from Zena. He knew she wasn't kidnapped or in danger. He knew deep down inside he's the cause of his fiancé leaving with no words. He could only imagine if the shoe was on the other foot, he knew he'd be hurt too. Steven decided to let her come back when the time is right instead of waiting around. As Steven was getting dressed for work, he got a text from Alisha. Steven had been ignoring Alisha, trying to distance himself from her because he wanted to make things right with Zena. In the text message, Alisha asked to see Steven. He finally decided to respond to let her know he's ready to cut ties. The two texted back and forth and he ended the conversation with "I'm going to stop by to pick up my card." Alisha began to smile; she knew she could reel him in with some pussy. Especially with the new lingerie she just picked up a few days ago with his card. Steven put his phone down and finished getting dressed. He began Crying to himself knowing he lost the only woman that loved him for who he was. Zena was there when he had nothing, not even a car to get back and forth to work. Zena and Steven shared her car at first before Steven landed a big job.

Steven could only think about Zena and his child at that moment as he broke down crying in his closet knowing that she was gone. Steven's thoughts:

"How could I let this happen."

"I didn't mean for all this to happen." "Stop playing victim Steve you did this shit."

"You lost your wife and family."

"I didn't think it would get this far."

# Chapter 10

*Temptation*

Alisha got dressed in the sexiest lingerie she could find that day at Victoria's Secret. She wanted to seduce Steve into changing his mind about stepping back from her. Alisha knew this day would come.

Luckily for her it fell on the day she was ovulating. She knew she could get Steven to come over. And once he saw her body in that lingerie oiled and ready he couldn't resist the temptation that was to come. While Steven was on his way to Alisha's house, he received a call from Rachel. Steven ignored her call but began to feel bad because he knew that he had her open and hadn't spoken to her since the last night they went out. Steven pulls over in his Mercedes and contemplates on calling Rachel back. He finally decided to give her a call once he noticed the three dots appearing in the text messages, meaning she was sending him a lengthy message. Steven loosens his tie as the phone rings. He starts to get nervous because he doesn't have an explanation as to why he hasn't spoken to her. Rachel answered the phone, From the hello in her voice Steven could tell she was pissed off. Steven begged for forgiveness and offered her another date to talk things over and explain himself. Rachel accepted the offer because she was still in a daze from their date previously. She couldn't stay mad at Steven for too long she figured he'd have a good explanation. Steven ended the call and drove off to Alisha's house to retrieve his belongings. He walked up to her door knocking on it a few times waiting for Alisha to answer.

Alisha opens the door with a black sparkly lingerie set on, that made Steven do a double take at her. Steven knew he couldn't resist the temptation that Alisha what's throwing at him, but he found a way to snap out of his lustful daze that was taking over him. Steven stopped at the door and told her that he didn't want to come in, he just wants his card. "Well, if you want it come get it", she replied as she seductively played with the card and stuffed it in her lingerie. "Look, not now Alisha, I have to get to work and as I said on the phone this thing, we have is over." Steven said in a stern voice. "I guess you wanna finally go home to that boring bitch huh. You know just like I do she can't suck that dick like me." she replied in a lustful way as she began to feel on Steven penis. "Hey! Hey! Hey! Hey! stop, Alisha chill we can't do this, and stop speaking on my fiancé, at least she could give me a kid." Steven said. Alisha grew furious and began to hit Steven. He knew that was a low blow. Alisha wants kids but can't produce them she had several miscarriages. She grabbed the card out of her lingerie top and threw it at him. "Fuck you and that basic bitch, we ain't over till I say we over mother fucker."

*BOOM!*

Alisha slams the door in Steven's face. He turns towards his car and gets in shaking his head at what just happened before he pulled off.

Chapter 11

## What's Wrong?

Zena laid in the hospital all she could think about was losing her child. She couldn't believe her baby was gone from her overreacting to Steven cheating. Zena was becoming depressed with the many thoughts that began to take over her mind. The nurse from the previous night was assigned to Zena again the next day. As she enters the room, she notices the look of defeat on Zena's face. She embraced her with a friendly hug and starts a conversation with her to change her mood. Once the nurse got Zena to smile a few times, joking with her she continued back to her job checking her vitals before releasing her back home. The nurse noticed the paper that had the therapist number written down and asked Zena if she had given any thought about calling her. Zena responded in an unsure manner, but eventually said yes, she would call as she put her clothes on. "Here, take these every 3 to 4 hours for pain, and don't forget to call Ms. Whitmoor she's really good with these matters," the nurse said to Zena as she wheeled her out of the room. "Do you have someone coming to get you?" the nurse asked, "I'm just going to catch an uber home, girl, I'll be fine." Zena realizes she doesn't have her phone to order a ride home, so she sighs at the thought of having to call Steven for a ride. She wasn't ready to have a conversation with him. Zena asks the nurse to use her phone to call a ride home. She starts to dial Steven's number and stops mid dial as she has flashbacks of the moaning and grunting, she heard that started these unfortunate events. She finally gets through to him, "Hello Steven I'm at Grace hospital and need a ride home I'll be waiting out front." Zena hung the phone up without waiting on him to respond. She didn't care what he had going on at that moment.

She didn't even want to hear his voice.

Steven got up from his desk with a sense of urgency starling his co-workers. They wondered why he rushed leaving the office so fast. Steven was so in a hurry he didn't even notice he left his keys in his desk. He had to run back inside to get them as his coworkers continued to wonder what was going on. He finds his keys and heads towards the door again but this time he is interrupted by his boss. "What's the rush Steven?" he asked, " I think my fiancé is having the baby". Congrats everyone in the office began shouting. "Thanks everyone, look, I'll zoom call you all once I make it there." Steven rushed back out of the office, got in his car and drove down 94 freeway headed towards Detroit. On his way to Zena all he could think about was her and the baby, he began to smile thinking of his beautiful baby. Steven thought she heard everything he and Rachel did and wasn't talking to him, but all this time it was because she was in the hospital. He then started to frown as his mind started racing.

"I wonder why she didn't call me and tell me she was

*having the baby?" "What if she didn't have the baby." "Damn did she have a heart attack, or some shit and they didn't know how to reach me?"*

*"Shit, I'm not sure, but I'm about to*

*find out"*, he said to himself as he pulled up to the hospital driveway looking out the Window for Zena. As he got closer, he sees Zena in a wheelchair not holding a baby so now he was really confused. He got out of the car and ran over to Zena to give her a hug, but she brushed past him, rolling her eyes as she opened the door and got in. Steven walked back over to the driver side of the car and got in. He looked over at Zena and asked if she was ok. Zena responded "mhmhmh, I'm good" Steven could tell something was off, he thought back. She must've of had a heart attack or something over hearing the sex him and Rachel had based off of the looks that she was given him. Zena kept side eyeing him causing him to keep his head straight on the road scared to say the wrong thing to her, so they rode home in silence with thick tension in the air.

Chapter 12

*Blast From The Past*

Rachel was wrapping up with her last client, walking her out the door, when her office phone started to ring. "Hello, you've reached Rachel Whitmoor, how may I help you?"
"Hi, yes my name is Zena Meyers I was given your number by a nurse at Grace hospital. She said your good to talk to about relationships." "Yes, Nurse

Terry told me you would be calling. It's the end of the day for me now and I'm booked up until Thursday, how does Friday at 9am sound?"

"Yes, that works out great for me," Zena replied.

Zena took down the address at the end of the call. When she hung up the phone, she took deep breath of fresh air feeling better about going to get some help. Rachel walked out of her office and to her surprise she saw her ex-boyfriend waiting by her car holding roses. She approached him with an evil look on her face asking him "why are you still trying?" Rachel and her ex-boyfriend broke up about 6 months ago. She caught him cheating with someone from his job. She was surprising him by bringing him lunch. She walked into his office to see him when she opened the door, she saw John and his former assistant kissing on top of his desk. The sight took a few months to finally leave Rachel thoughts before she could move on. It hurt her worse because she vented to him about everything her previous ex had put her through, and he turned around and did the same thing. She got over it eventually, using some of her own techniques she taught to her clients. Rachel snatches the flowers out of John's hand and throws them at his feet, smacking him one last time before getting in her Mercedes and pulling off. While on her way home she began to go into deep thought:

*"God, I hate narcissistic ass men."*

"Please don't let steven be one, God." "I wonder has he been keeping it real with me."

Curiosity starts to take over Rachel's mind as she pulls to the side of the road reaching in her Gucci bag for her phone. After retrieving her cell phone, she scrolls to Steven's name and begins to send him a message, in the middle of texting she gets a call from Steven. She picked the phone up on the first ring, fumbling the phone because she wasn't expecting his call. Steven called her just to confirm their date for the evening, he was trying to get back on Rachels good side proving that she can still trust him and his word, because the last time he went days without speaking to her. She hung the phone up blushing feeling as if that call was a sign from God, seeing how she was just thinking of him at that moment.

## Chapter 13
*"J"*

Alisha sat on her couch smoking a blunt thinking about the words that Steven said to her.

*"Who the fuck he thinks he is?"*

"The audacity of him to throw up the fact I can't have kids."

"He only with her for a kid, he was just trying to leave her before he found out about that baby."

"I should tell the bitch what's going on."

By the end of her blunt she came to the conclusion that it was time to make Steven jealous and feel how she felt. She got up from the couch and headed towards her bedroom to get dressed for the day. Alisha wanted to grab some attention, she looked in her closet and wandered through her clothes and came across a Versace Jumpsuit that complemented her curves well. She grabbed her Versace heels and bag that matched the jumpsuit, before heading to the

master bathroom in her house. After Alisha steps out of her shower, her phone begins to buzz, it's a call from Steven. She declines the call and continues to get dressed. Alisha walks out of her house and heads towards her car, before starting the car she sits there and thought to herself.
"Where should I go?"
"Where are all the ballers at, I ain't been out in a while, I

*don't even know where to start."*

Alisha sat in her car another 5 minutes, until it came to her that she could call her girl Trina. Trina and Alisha have been best friends for over 10 years. Trina hates Steven because she knows he's a dog and no good for her friend. No matter how many times she talks to her about Steven, Alisha never listens.

Alisha gets through to Trina and convinces her to go out. Trina suggests they should go to a dayshift at Truth Gentlemen's club, that's where guys her speed hung out. She backs out of her Driveway in her Mercedes and heads toward the strip club. When she arrived, she noticed Bentleys, Mercedes, Jaguars, Maybachs and a variety of other expensive cars in the valet area. Alisha knew with her game and body she could get any man she wanted with the snap of her fingers. She exited her car and was greeted by the valet driver. She paid and tipped him before heading inside. When Alisha walked inside the club, she saw Trina sitting in a booth drinking a bottle of 1942 Don Julio and smoking hookah. Next to her was a booth of four guys sitting down and three other guys standing around them throwing wads of money at the dancer on stage, It was exciting to her. Alisha walked up to the booth with Trina and started smiling telling her how "lit this place looks" as she sat down pouring herself a shot of 1942. The two continued having a good time ordering food and singles to get dances from the strippers.

She caught the attention of one of the guys throwing money when she walked in. He walked over to their booth signaling the thickest dancers to come over to their section. Once the dancers arrived, he whispered in their ear telling them to give her friend a few dances while he talked to the other one. The strippers began to dance on Trina. She started slapping them on their ass while Alisha sat back laughing and the guy as well. He walked over to Alisha and told her "This is courtesy of the mob, I wanted to talk to you, but I didn't want your friend cockblocking." The two laughed and joked like old friends, introducing each other and taking shots. By the end of the conversation, he asked for her number.  To her surprise Trina was all for it smiling at her nodding her head signaling her to do it, all the while smacking the dancers on the booty. While exchanging numbers with the new guy, Steven called her phone again, making her fumble her phone dropping it on the table. She quickly grabbed it and denied his call smoothly without the new guy seeing it. Alisha retrieves her phone and takes down his number. She was so nervous and buzzing from the shots she forgot his name. "Just save it Under "J from the club" he says to her. After J walked away the ladies embraced at what just took place. Trina told her about J and how he was one of the biggest pill lords around the city. Bringing a smile on Alisha's face because that's the lifestyle she is used to before meeting Steven. That smile quickly went away when she received a text from Steven saying, *"Stop playing with me and answer your phone!"* then another text comes through *"look, baby I'm sorry about what I said."* She put her phone down and it rang again, another call from Steven. She finally answers and before she could say anything Steven said, "I'm on my way to Truth since you don't wanna talk on the phone." Alisha told Trina it was time for her to go. She had an emergency she needs to attend to as she gets up from the booth rushing out the door. She got to the door waiting for the Valet guy to bring her car around. J walked up to her and asked. "Is everything ok? You getting outta here kinda fast." Alisha responded nervously looking around for her car, then back at the entrance to make sure Steven wasn't pulling up, before she gave J a hug. "Everything is fine. You can go back inside the club, baby, my car is pulling up now." Alisha got in her car headed towards her house turning off her location that she shared with steven before pulling off into traffic.

Chapter 14

## Deceit

"I can't believe my baby is gone." Zena cried over and over sitting in the middle of her baby's bedroom. "How could I have let this happen?" She asked herself. Zena got up from the floor wiping large tears from her eyes. She glanced over her left shoulder and saw a picture of Herself and Steven. Zena took the picture off the wall admiring how happy they used to be, tears began to roll down her cheek. Zena wipes the tears away then throws the picture frame against the wall shattering the glass that protected the picture. She headed towards her bedroom bursting through the door, flopping down on her bed wondering where she could have gone wrong. Zena laid in bed staring at the ceiling while her mind drifted away with guilt.

*"Was it my cooking?"*
*"I did everything for that man."*
*"We had sex all the time, I know I wasn't lacking in bedroom." "Is this my Karma?"*

Zena thought of that business card that was in Steven's wallet. "I wonder is that who's he been with?"

Zena got upset at herself for moving fast and not getting a chance to read the card that night. After having so many thoughts running through her mind, she decided it was time to break out of her depression and get back to her normal self. She realized crying was not solving anything. She goes toward her bedroom door then downstairs towards the kitchen to fix dinner. Zena figured it was time to talk with Steven and let him know everything. Zena picks up her phone and texted Steven letting him know dinner will be done by 8:30 and they needed to have a talk. Steven replied: *"Ok."* and she began to prepare for dinner.

Steven put his phone down after texting Zena back and sat inside his drop top BMW waiting for Rachel to arrive.

His phone rings: *Alisha*, Steven denies the call because he didn't want to take that bad energy with him into the restaurant before meeting with Rachel. Alisha sends him a text message: *"That was unfair for you to spoil my fun and not be at my house making up for it."* Steven texted back: *"I will call you later."* After sending that text message he lifted his head and saw Rachel pulling into the lot. He was so eager to get out of his car, he didn't notice he left his car key inside of the cup holder. Rachel gets out of her Mercedes and the first thing he saw was her attire. Steven is weak for a classy dressing woman that smells good. Rachel headed over to him with her model walk as her YSL heels clicked across the pavement. Her skintight dress complemented her C cup breasts and curvy waist. Steven said to himself *"Damn I almost let that go, I'm tripping."* The two embraced with tight hugs and pecked kisses on each other's lips as if it had been years since they last saw one another. They headed towards the restaurant, hand in hand. As they began their evening Steven ordered 2 rounds of Dusse for them, while Rachel checked out the menu. She finally decided on lamb chops, lobster mac and asparagus, so did Steven. The two had a conversation about why Steven went missing for a few days, he made up some lie. Steven explained his made-up story well enough for Rachel to believe him. After dinner Steven and Rachel decided to leave and go to her place to hang out for a while. When he arrived at Rachel's house, he noticed that it was 9:40 pm and he hadn't received a call or text from Zena yet. He figured she was asleep by now. Steven gets out of the car walking up to Rachel's door, again, holding hands and giggling like school kids. He notices his phone vibrate from a call. Once Rachel opened the door Steven looked down at his phone and saw he had an incoming call from Zena. He shook his head knowing she would be pissed that he missed dinner and more importantly the conversation. He was dying to figure out what she wanted to say. Steven walked in and thought of a way he could get out of this without raising any red flags. He sat on the couch and began to act as if his stomach was hurting from dinner. Rachel notices a discomforting look on his face and asks, "Do you need anything?" Steven replied, "You know what? My stomach is tripping might've been those drinks or dinner, let me get going. Can I see you tomorrow?" he asked. "Sure." Rachel replied giving him a confused look as if she didn't have a bathroom at her home. They hugged each other, and Steven jetted to his car and pulled off burning rubber to Get home.

## Chapter 15

*Love Lost*

Alisha sat on her love seat in her woman cave smoking a blunt. She was talking on speaker phone with Trina about the fun they had the night before. After their conversation, Alisha continued to smoke her blunt daydreaming of the man she met at the club. Alisha was so used to dealing with Steven she forgot how good other men looked and how nice they treated her because of her looks. Alisha was getting wet thinking of how good his sex probably is. She could not resist the temptation. She grabbed her rose toy, opened her silk robe and began to spread her legs putting the rose on her clitoris, moaning and feeling on her breast. Alisha squirted from the orgasm she just gave herself. She decided it was time to forget all about Steven and give J a call. She felt guilty at first but told herself "There's nothing to be guilty about because I'm no longer in a relationship. Steven is going back to his fiancé." Alisha built up enough courage to call J, but to her surprise the phone went to voicemail. Alisha threw her phone on the bed and headed towards the shower to clean off.

Steven pulls into his driveway nervous about the conversation Zena wants to have with him. He walked in and saw his dinner on the table. He looked at the other end of the table and didn't see Zenas plate. He turned around to close the door and was startled at Zena sitting on the couch giving him a death stare drinking wine. "What are you doing sitting in the dark, and why are you drinking wine? "That should be the least of your worries Steve." Zena replied. Steven removed his red bottom dress shoes and Ralph Lauren peacoat and headed towards the living room.

"Don't you wanna eat, or did she feed you already?" Zena said in a sarcastic tone. "Who are you talking about baby? Is this what you wanted to talk about?" He asked as if he was shocked, but he knew exactly who Zena was talking about. Listen Steven I'm going to make this as short as possible. "I heard you having sex with somebody." Zena shouted

"Huh, wha what are you talking about baby"? Steven replied.

The two were in a heated argument, when Zena began getting weak from the prior procedure. Steven rushed over to her "Are you ok? Is it the baby?" He asked, concerned for a baby that was no longer there. "No Steven, move get off of me!" Zena replied.

"Look Steven, I know you lying, I heard you and the bitch fucking and I lost the baby."

Steven dropped to his knees in disbelief and started to cry holding Zena by the leg pleading how sorry he was. Zena pushed him off her. "You said I love you, and I said it too the only difference is I didn't lie to you." Zena said firmly, before storming toward the 210 front door. She grabbed her car key and purse, she needed to take a drive to clear her mind. Slamming the door on her way out. Steven got off the floor and sat in the chair with his hands to his face crying about the loss of his baby and possibly the woman he loved.

Chapter 16

*Regret*

Meanwhile back at home in her woman cave Alisha laid in her bed mind racing. She was torn between moving on from Steven or sticking it out with him for security. Alisha was not sure if any man would put up with her spoiled ways, and if another man would have as much money as Steven and be as generous. She battled with the thoughts throughout the night.

The next day Alisha woke up from a text that was sent out at 2am. She realized it was from J's phone number. Alisha jumped out of bed and fumbles her phone shocked that J responded. Alisha sat her phone down to brush her teeth but was interrupted by a phone call from Steven. She answers the phone expecting to hear Steve saying something about the other day, but instead she was awestruck hearing Steven crying on saying "My baby is gone Alisha."

No matter what Steven and Alisha went through he could always vent to her and she would listen, without responding or cutting him off. Which made him talk even more, sometimes for hours. This was also another reason it was hard for Steven to let go of Alisha; he felt more open with her than any other woman. She just could not have kids and that's something Steven always wanted. Alisha felt bad for Steven, she never seen him this hurt out of all the years they've known each other. Steven asked if he could come see her, but Alisha wasn't sure how to respond. She cared for Steven, but she grew tired of him not taking her serious enough to be with her. Alisha told Steven she had some important things to take care of that morning so he couldn't come over at the time. Alisha felt bad about lying to Steven, but she didn't care because he lies to her at times. Alisha told Steven she would give him a call once she's done, with her day. Alisha scrolled back to J's number and seen he sent a message to her saying he wants to meet for brunch this afternoon. She smiled, and does a little happy dance headed towards her closet to get dressed for the day.

Steven sat in his lazy boy chair with his feet up in disbelief of what his actions had caused. Steven called off work and turned his phone on do not disturb. He didn't feel obligated to talk to anyone at that moment.

Steven grew up an only child, he was adopted by a wealthy black family that had no kids. Stevens adopted mom was like Alisha, she couldn't have children of her own. Adopting Steven was the highlight of her life. They gave him any and everything a kid could want. When he turned 18, they were killed in a crash leaving everything behind to Steven. Steven was hurting mentally from losing his parents, so he distanced himself for a while from everyone. That was his coping mechanism before meeting Alisha. She was the first woman he could talk to about anything. Their relationship took a turn after one of her routine doctor's appointments and she found out she couldn't have kids. Steven ended up going bankrupt because he didn't have the knowledge to maintain the lifestyle he was living. That's when he met Zena.

Zena at the time was a financial advisor, she helped Steven fix his credit and got him out of debt that his parents left behind which fell on him. Zena and Steven dated for some time before he finally asked to be with her. After finding out she was pregnant Steven asked her to marry him and Zena happily said yes. Zena had a miscarriage with their first child when she was only 4 weeks along. They didn't lose hope then. Steven wanted to try for another one and so did Zena. Steven blamed himself over and over knowing he messed up this time around and that he caused her so much hurt that she lost this baby too. This was Stevens first time getting caught cheating so he wasn't sure how things would pan out between him and Zena.

Alisha walked back into her room getting herself together to go to brunch with J. She was indecisive on what to wear. She knew J was a big-time drug dealer, so she didn't want to look basic. She wanted his eyes to pop when he saw her again. Alisha dug deep in her closet and found some high waist jeans and a black off the shoulder shirt that complemented her tattoos. She grabbed her black and brown LV heels and purse to match. Alisha was now dressed and ready to see J, before heading out the door she grabbed her cartier sunglasses and Mercedes car key from the table. J and

Alisha Met at a nice brunch spot that serves mimosas as soon as you walk in the door. The two embraced each other with a hug before being seated by their waitress. During their date Alisha kept her phone in her purse to keep J from seeing that Steven was calling like a mad man. She was Relaxed knowing her location was turned off. J was getting ready to leave soon because he had some plays in the street to make, which also eased Alisha because she could finally call Steven back and see what he wanted. After brunch J and Alisha walked out of the restaurant holding hands, J asks Alisha "When am I seeing you again?" "Later." Alisha responded. J leaned in and gave Alisha a kiss and Alisha kissed back. The two hugged and kissed for a minute before J's phone went off from his supplier so he took the call and walked off while Alisha got in her car. Alisha sat in her car smiling and thinking what if, before starting her car she said to herself *"Girl what did you just get yourself into?"*

# Chapter 17

*Zena Meets Rachel*

Zena walked into her house surprised to see Steven sitting in the same spot he was sitting in when she left. Steven woke up and ran to Zena's feet begging for forgiveness, but all Zena could do was shake her head and push him off her. She headed straight to her room to get herself together for her first therapy session with Rachel that day.

Back at her office Rachel was in a session with her client when she got an unexpected text from Steven saying he needed to talk. Rachel's mind started to race causing her to not fully hear what her client was saying. Her client realized Rachel wasn't fully paying attention because her energy shifted from being focused and asking questions, to her tapping her pen on her chair repeatedly, and eyes wondering around the room. Rachel snaps out of her own thoughts and back into her client once she realized her client had stopped talking and was giving her a look as if she wanted to leave. Rachel finished her session and called Steven back to see what was on his mind. Steven missed her call because he turned his phone on silent mode, while Zena was still in the house. Rachel started to question if things were ok with Steven. He sent a text telling her he would call her back and give him a minute. Zena grabbed her car keys and headed for the door, on her way-out Steven said, "I'm sorry," causing Zena to slam the door as she headed towards the driveway. Zena arrived at her session and sat in her car talking to herself before she went inside. *"Ok I'm here now, time to start healing Zena."* She got out of her Porsche truck and walked into Rachels office being greeted by her assistant. Zena told the woman she was there to see Rachel Whitmoor. The assistant called Rachel and told her that her next client has arrived. Rachel walked up front and greeted Zena "Hello beautiful you can follow me to my office." Zena sat down and introduced herself and so did Rachel. Rachel had a way with making people feel comfortable enough to share their darkest moments with her, that was her job. Rachel shared her background and life experiences and what made her qualified to help Zena with her issues. Zena began to vent her problems away. For privacy reasons Zena didn't speak the name of the person she was venting about she referred to him as "My Childs Father. After Zena told Rachel most of her issues. Rachel gave her some mental exercises to help her cope with the loss of her baby and her cheating child's father. In the midst of talking Rachel gets a call on her cell phone from Steven. She stops exchanging with Zena, gets up and tells her "Excuse me, this is an important call I must take." As she walked into the hallway. She spoke with Steven "Hey I'm in the middle of a session and I need to call you back." Rachel returned apologizing for interrupting their session. Zena questioned her "Are you single or married?" Rachel responded "Just dating this wonderful guy right now nothing serious. Why'd you ask that?" " They all ain't shit sis, you haven't learned that by now? I know I'm not your only client that has relationship problems. Just take your time don't rush anything." Zena informed her. "Thank you, I will keep that in mind."

Rachel replied. "Well, how about we set you up for next week." Rachel says to Zena. Zena gets her next appointment from Rachel's assistant and walks towards the door. Rachel yells "Hey wait, take my card, call me any time my office and cell number are on here." Zena takes the card and put it in her purse. She looks at the shelf behind Rachel and notices she has crystals.

Zena asks, "why do you have those crystals just laying around." Rachel gets up from her desk and walks over to the shelf picking up 3 crystals explains their meaning. "These are called Healing crystals."

"This Pink one is called a rose quartz it's all about love, it helps restore trust and harmony in all different kinds of relationships improving their close connections."

"This turquoise one has powers that are said to help heal the mind, body, and soul."

"Then you got this brown one this is my favorite it's called the Tigers eye. Its purpose is to help guide you to harmony and balance to help your career and conscious decisions making."

"Wow, you really know your shit girl. Do you really believe these work, Now I'm interested" Zena says. Rachel wrote down an address and told Zena to stop by and pick up a few crystals and try them for herself. Zena thanked her and walked out of the office, feeling refreshed.

Rachel rushed back to her phone to give Steven a call,

but it went to voicemail. Rachel threw her phone on top of her desk out of frustration.

## Chapter 18

*"Until a man finds himself, he will destroy everything he touches"*

 Days had gone by, and Steven decided it was time to pull himself together. He realized it was Sunday, so he thought it was a good idea to go to church and ask for forgiveness. Steven showered and grabbed his Armani suit and dress shoes out of his closet, he wore his gold day date Rolex and put on his diamond cross pendant. Steven parked his Rolls Royce in front of the church and walked inside. The service had already started, the pastor was already up preaching. The Sermon that Sunday just so happened to be about loving yourself and forgiving others. About 45 minutes into the service. Steven started to feel such conviction as if the pastor was speaking directly to him. Steven knew it was just his guilty conscience eating him up on the inside. After the service was over Steven approached the pastor and asked if he could speak with him alone. Steven and the pastor walked to the back of the church and introduced themselves. After the introduction Steven told the pastor what's been going on in his life and asked him for the best Godly advice instead of leaning to his own understanding. The pastor told Steven "Until a man finds himself, he will destroy everything he touches." For the first time everything made sense to steven. He thanked the pastor for the advice and asked him could he pray with him. The minister told him to lift his hands and repeat after him. Steven felt a weight being lifted off his shoulder when he left church. His new problem was trying to figure out a way to cut everybody off. He had deep soul ties and long-lasting friendships with these women, it wasn't going to be easy. Steven figured his first stop would be to Alisha since he knows she's going to be the most difficult. Steven sat in his Rolls Royce outside of the church still trying to figure out the words to say to Alisha without things getting out of hand. He felt Zena should be the last to be cut off He knows that he owes her so much and won't be able find the words to tell Zena that he wants to focus on himself. He knows it won't be the news she wants to hear especially after losing their child. Steven figured he needed a drink to help ease his mind. Although he just left church, he thought God would understand that he needed a drink to help clear his mind from this mess he created. Steven headed to the nearest bar he could find on that side of town.

After about 4 shots and 2 Long Islands Steven was ready to face what was to come with Alisha.

## Chapter 19

*What Did You Do?*

That afternoon Alisha and J were laying in her bed from the previous night out. J took Alisha to a night club and spent over 5 thousand dollars on bottles and dancers for their section. After leaving the club the two were pissy drunk. Alisha was woken up from J's phone going off thinking it was hers. Alisha almost screamed when she seen J laying in her bed forgetting he stayed over. Alisha was used to sleeping with Steven, so to see a new face in her bed shocked her. Alisha came back to her senses greeting J with a kiss rubbing his baller belly saying, "good morning baby." J kissed her back as they laid their talking about what a night they had. J started rubbing his hands on Alisha's ass getting turned on by her curves. J didn't get a chance to have sex with Alisha last night because they were both too drunk to function. He Practically had to carry her inside her home.

Alisha felt J's dick getting hard, she got aroused causing her pussy lips to tingle. Alisha climbed on top of J and they kissed each other passionately. J slide his underwear off she felt how rock hard his dick was pressed against her swollen pussy lips. She continued to kiss on his neck and his chest. J couldn't handle the foreplay Alisha was offering, he was too eager to feel the inside of her pussy. Her juices dripped on his dick from her grinding on it. He lifted her thigh and slid his dick inside of Alisha. She got on her feet in a squatting position. She bounced up and down on J's dick while he smacked her ass. He grabbed her by her throat and told her "This pussy is mine now." Hearing those words turned Alisha on even more she was ready for her favorite position. Alisha stopped riding J's dick and got on her knees, bent over arching her back with her ass in the air. J got up and got behind Alisha, before putting his dick inside of her he stuck two fingers inside of her pussy then took his other hand and stuck his thumb inside of her ass and played with her. Alisha began to squirt all over J's hand and her bed while she screamed from it feeling so good. J slides his dick inside of Alisha while she was still doggy style. He slaps her ass while stroking her pussy. Alisha begins to squirt again turning J on. Making his dick harder inside of Alisha's pussy. She screams out "Fuck me baby, this your pussy now."

Steven pulls up to Alisha's house and sits in his car contemplating on if he is ready to cut off his long-term friend. He talked to himself about the pros and cons of how this would affect him, but he was willing to give it up. Steven was buzzing from the Long Islands and shots and started to think about Alisha's pussy. He told himself he would fuck one more time and that would be the end. Steven knew Alisha liked to smoke weed so he reached in his bag and grabbed some "cookie" weed and rolled a blunt in a dark stout back wood, that was her favorite flavor. He figured the conversation would be calm if they both were smoking while talking. After rolling up Steven noticed a Black Jaguar in Alisha's driveway and wondered who it could be because he knew only Trina came over, but she drove an Escalade. Steven reached back inside his duffel bag and grabbed his .45 tucking it in his waistline before exiting his car. Steven walked up to the door turned the knob, but it was locked. He tried using his key but to his surprise Alisha had changed her locks. Steven to grew Frustrated. He looked under her flowerpot where she normally keeps her spare key and to his surprise the new key was there.

Steven went inside and noticed a pair of Prada gyms shoes at the door which were a little too big to be Alisha's. He quietly closed the door and grab his gun from his waistline. Steven crept downstairs peeping around to see what was going on. He heard moaning coming from upstairs. He creeps up the stairs so no one could hear him and heads towards Alisha's room where the moaning and grunting was coming from. Steven cocked his pistol back putting one bullet in the chamber and prepared himself to go inside. Steven counts to three and bursts into the room kicking the door. Steven lifts his Gun and freezes in shock as he sees Alisha sucking J's dick on her knees. J pushes Alisha out the way and goes to reach for his gun, *"Bang"*

"Bang" "Bang" "Bang", Steven lets off four shots into J's chest. Alisha screams in shock. "What have you done Steven?" Alisha screams out over and over. Steven stood in shock to what just took place. With his gun still lifted he stared at J while he bled out. "What are you here for Steven? You just killed this man. Steven say something." she screamed out. Steven blanked out of his dazed and looked over at Alisha with his gun still pointed at J and told her "This stays between us right, right?" he screamed. "Yes Steven, yes this is between us." she said to him as she was crying and scared as to what Steven was going to do next. She never saw this side of him; she knew Steven had anger issues, but not to this extreme. Steven paced back and forth talking to himself thinking out loud on what to do. The curiosity killed Alisha, so she asked, "So what are we going to do Steven?"

"Get yourself cleaned up and slip some clothes on we bout to bury this nigga."

Chapter 20

*What To Do?*

Rachel woke up from her nap to a phone call from Zena, she was excited to tell her she was at the crystal shop she gave her the address to. Rachel sat up and talked with Zena as she looked through the store selection of crystals amazed at the texture of the citrine stone sitting on the shelf. Rachel told Zena to let her heart and mind flow and she will pick the right stones.

Rachel Looked at the clock on the wall jumping up realizing

The store was closing early today because it was the weekend. Rachel ended the call. She jumped up from her couch running to her room to get dressed. After a few minutes Rachel realized she hadn't heard from Steven. She slowed down getting dressed and thought to herself: *what is really going on with him?* She slipped into her jeans and hooked her bra together looking over at her phone hoping it would ring. Rachel did not want to seem like a pest calling him so much, but she needed to know what was really going on with him. Rachel stopped getting dressed and walked over to her phone, she didn't hesitate like any other time she called him. Steven denied the phone call, but texted back *"I'll call you once I'm done, we really need to talk."* Rachel did not like the sound of that, she sat her phone back down and continued getting dressed.

Rachel heads out her front door but gets pushed against the wall by her ex holding her arms up forming the letter "Y". "Get off of me Raheem" she screamed. Raheem grew irritated trying every possible way to get Rachel back, but every time he tried, she brushed him off. Raheem demanded that she take him back and let him fix everything. Rachel screamed and kick at him. She kneed him in his balls causing him to grunt and double over in pain. This made it easy for her to pepper spray him before he could recover. Rachel ran back inside slamming the door and locking all the locks she ran upstairs and grabbed the gun her dad gave her. She returned to the door to check and see if he was still there, but Raheem had driven off crashing trash cans and bumping cars because he couldn't see from the pepper spray in his eyes. Rachel left and went to the local police station to file a police report and get a restraining order on

Raheem. Once leaving the police station Rachel looked at her Rolex and realized the store was closing in 10 minutes. She was so frustrated she slammed her car door. After sitting in the police stations parking lot looking up stores on google. Rachel finally decided to give up and try again tomorrow.

Back at the Crystal store Zena decided to buy 4 stones. The first one was a 268 clear quartz which can help you manifest a higher state of consciousness. The second was an Amazonite stone, its purpose is to bring prosperity & Healing. The third, a Celestine stone which brings harmony and balance, it also helps maintain inner peace. The last Crystal Zena purchased was a blue calcite which brings creativity and improves mental clarity.

Zena left the store anxious to see what the crystals would bring into her life. She was desperately searching for a way to heal her broken heart before she made a decision that would land her in jail. When Zena made it home, she checked her cell phone to see if she had any missed calls from Steven because hadn't been home all day. She starts to dial his number but gets a call from

Rachel instead. "Hey, I was just checking on you, which crystals did you decide to buy from the store?" Rachel questioned. They talked on the phone for about an hour which ended with Rachel inviting Zena over for a lady's night. Zena accepted the offer and told her she would see her later before hanging up. Rachel pulled off from a store she found still open 27 minutes away from her home. During her ride home Rachel received a call from an unknown number. Normally she doesn't answer unknown numbers, most times is Raheem's crazy ass, she thought maybe it was Steven, so she answered the call. To her surprise it was her doctor "Hello I'm looking for Rachel Whitmoor." the voice on the other end of the phone said. "Hello this is Rachel." Ms. Whitmoor this is Dr Thomas I have some sensitive information to share with you can you tell me your date of birth?" Rachel gave her date of birth to her physician and held her breath. She was unsure of what the doctor could possibly want to tell her. "I called to inform you of the results from your routine pregnancy test were positive, your pregnant. Rachel stripped her car's tires burning rubber as she pulled over to the side of the road. "I'm what?" she shouted. Rachel hung the phone up screaming to the top of her lungs and punching the steering wheel. Rachel was upset because she was 2 months along which led back to Raheem, because she just met Steven a few weeks ago. Rachel pulled off from the side of the road crying and upset with herself. She wondered why Raheem has been so trying so hard to get back with her. Rachel's mind was blown because she thought they were being careful, she made Raheem pull out every time. Rachel arrived home and sat in her driveway thinking if she should tell Raheem or just get rid of it because she wanted to focus on a relationship with Steven. After overthinking so much Rachel started to cry again, she got out of her car and walked inside with her wine and few groceries. Rachel made it inside she sat everything down and took off her coat and headed towards the wine bottle, taking the top off and drinking it straight from the bottle.

Chapter 21

*Do You Trust Me*

Steven and Alisha wrapped sheets around J's body so they could carry him to the trunk of his car. Steven picked J up off the floor and through his body over his shoulder and carried him to the car. Once Steven had J's body in the trunk, he went back inside to get cleaned up. J's blood had dripped all over his shirt and pants. Steven walked to the master bedroom and opened the dresser that Alisha gave him for his clothes. He grabbed some underwear and a T-shirt, then headed over to the closet and grabbed a Nike jogging suit before taking a shower. While

Steven was in the bathroom Alisha was panicking, pacing the floor talking to herself. "What the fuck just happened?" "I can't believe this just happened." "I hope he has a plan." Alisha continued to pace the floor talking to herself. She stopped mid step when she noticed there was blood on her carpet. Alisha ran downstairs to the kitchen to retrieve some stain remover and a towel to clean the blood. While cleaning the blood Alisha's mind was racing was stopped scrubbing the floor when she thought about J's phone possibly being Pinged back to her house. Alisha could not take her thoughts anymore. She burst into the bathroom scaring Steven while he was in the shower, he almost fell. "What the fuck Alisha?" he screamed.

"Steven, they are going to ping his phone back to my house. What are we going to do?" Steven turned the water off and stepped out of the shower grabbing his towel. "Relax Alisha, I'm going to handle it." he responded. Steven got dressed and told Alisha to meet him in the kitchen so they can discuss the game plan. "Look Alisha, if the police come asking questions or says his phone pinged back here. Then you tell them you were just buying weed from him. He came by y'all smoked and went out for drinks. He dropped you off afterwards because you were too drunk to drive, and you haven't heard from him since."

"Ok got it, so what are we going to do with his body?" Alisha replied. "We're gonna take him out to Romeo. You gonna follow me in my car while I drive his car." He shot back. "Steven, do you think this plan is going to work?" Steven got mad yelling and her blaming her for all of this. The two argued for 10 minutes. Alisha started crying again and Steven walked out the door slamming it before entering J's car. Alisha wiped her tears away talking to herself preparing for what she was about to do. She walked outside and got in Steven's car. She adjusted the seat to her height just before pulling off; Steven went first, and she followed. It was a 45-minute drive to Romeo, Michigan but Steven and Alisha finally reached their destination. It was an empty field next to a forest of trees. Steven opened the trunk and grabbed J's body out. He dragged him to the darkest area in the forest where a hole was already dug. Alisha's eyebrows raised in shock. She asked, "why is there a hole already dugout Steven?" before he could respond. A short man with a full beard and dirty clothes emerged from behind the trees greeting Steven. The two shook hands and Steven handed him an envelope filled with money. Steven told Alisha to wait in the car and they will handle the rest. Steven buried the body and walked back to his car while the short man drove off in J's car.

"Where is he going in his car? Do you trust him?" Alisha said to Steven

"Yes, I trust him, that's my uncle he worked for the mafia growing up, he knows what to do. He's gonna burn J's car up with all evidence. This is the last place

somebody would come to look." Steven says to Alisha". Steven left the scene thinking to himself. He drove for about 5 miles in silence before pulling over and talking to Alisha. "Look we in this together now, I gotta know I can trust you." steven says to Alisha"
"You can trust me Steven, I've been here for you since

day one, can I trust you though"?

Steven looked over at Alisha and said, "Yes you can trust me I did this for us."

"How did you know? Why did you come over without calling first?" Steven sat silent for a while because he knew he came over to break things off with Alisha. Now he's committed murder and feels obligated to Alisha because she has dirt on him that could put him in jail for ever if shit hits the fan. Steven said to her "I was coming to surprise you. I know things ended badly the other day. I just wanted to make it up to you." He pulled off shaking his head realizing how much deeper things are now between him and Alisha.

Chapter 22

## Lady's Night

Zena gathered her belongings that she was taking over to Rachel's house for their ladies' night. She doubled back to make sure she had everything. After packing her bag Zena made sure to grab her crystals on the way out the door. She put her bags in the car and closed the trunk. She walked towards her driver door looking down at her keys but stopped mid step and was startled to see Steven standing in front of her car. He walked around to her and asked: "Going somewhere?" "Yeah," she replied "I'm going to a friend's house to have ladies' night, drink wine and clear our minds. Seeing as you're the reason

My mind is so clouded." "Im sorry baby." steven begged for forgiveness. "Move Steven" Zena shouted as she got in her car and backed out of the driveway. She sped off without looking back at Steven who was waving goodbye to her. Steven stood outside and looked around the neighborhood taking in deep breaths of fresh air from the overwhelming day he's had. After thinking to himself for over an hour Steven looked down at his shoes and noticed blood on them from J's body. He walked inside to take a shower, but before going upstairs, he stopped inside the garage and grabbed some firewood from the shelf. He made his way back inside and walked over to the fireplace. Steven took off his clothes & shoes and placed them inside the fireplace, setting the logs on top of them before starting the fire. Steven stood and watched the last of the evidence burn away thinking to himself: *"I should've gotten Alisha clothes as well."*

Steven walked upstairs to the master bedroom and headed

towards his secret compartment in the floor. He pressed the code on the wall behind his bookshelf causing the floorboar ds to slide open. He placed the pistol that he killed J with inside of there. After closing his safe spot. Steven grabbed his underwear and walked over to the shower turning it on. He stepped in letting the water wash over his face and dreads he let out a deep sigh of relief from his wild day.

Zena arrived at Rachel's house; she was amazed at how nice her home looked on the outside. Rachel saw the headlights from Zena's car pulling into her driveway and opens the door waiting for her to get out of the car.

The two hugged and walked inside of Rachel's home. Zena was amazed at how beautiful Rachel had her home decorated. Rachel asked Zena if she'd like a tour, so she'd feel more welcome and know where everything was for the night. Zena fell in love with her home, her favorite room was Rachel's prayer room. It was filled with peace and crystals all around. Zena thought to herself *"I need to make a room like this."* After the tour Rachel and Zena walked into the kitchen, where Rachel had already prepared dinner. She had four different wine bottles to choose from. For dinner Rachel made spaghetti and garlic bread, which was one of Zena's favorite foods to make.

After dinner they headed towards the living room to watch tv and finish their drinks. They didn't realize how much they had been venting to each other, and time sped past them. There were only two bottles of wine left. Back at home Steven sat in his chair thinking to himself how his life has taken a crazy turn all because he wanted his cake and to eat it too. He looked down at his phone and saw a text from Alisha. He hesitated to respond because Alisha had texted him: *"I'm sorry,"* but he knew she was only sorry she got caught.

Steven decided to give Rachel a call and get some advice from a professional standpoint. Before calling, Steven felt the need to smoke a blunt before

explaining what's been going on with him.
Rachel and Zena were laughing and talking while watching "Coming of age 2," on amazon prime. Before they knew it they were down to their last bottle of wine. Once the movie went off Rachel excused herself to use the bathroom, she had a little too much wine. She got up and headed towards the bathroom while Zena opens

the last bottle filling both of their cups. In the midst of pouring their drinks Rachels cell phone starts to ring. Zena didn't pay any attention to it because she was buzzing from drinking so much. The phone stops ringing, as Rachel walks back into the living room flopping down on her couch feeling relieved. Rachel reaches for the remote and her phone starts to ring again, this time

Zena catches the name that appeared on Rachel's phone: *Steve with Heart eyes emoji*. "Hey baby, how are you feeling?" Rachel excused herself into the next room to talk. Seeing that name raised some suspicion, Zena's eyebrows raised. Rachel was buzzing and that caused her to be loud not knowing Zena was listening to her conversation. Rachel ended the phone call and sat back on the couch. She sat her phone on the table and asked Zena if she was hungry again, Zena replied "yes." Even though she wasn't hungry she knew that would be the perfect time to see if it was Steven that had called Rachel's phone. As she got up from the couch Zena leaned forward and grabbed Rachel's phone quickly scrolling to her last call. Zena dropped her wine glass on the floor, surprised to see it was actually Stevens' number that had called. Zena threw the phone back on the table and sat there in shock as Rachel came back with some spaghetti on a plate for them. "Oh, my goodness is everything ok? Let me get a towel and clean this up." Rachel said. As Rachel came back into the room got down on her hands and knees to clean the stain out of her carpet. Zena grabbed the wine bottle and cracked Rachel in the head causing the bottle to shatter and the remaining wine to spill all over the floor blending in with Rachel's blood. Zena quickly packed her things and ran out of the house towards her car. She burned rubber as she pulled off and headed towards Steven.

To be continued…….

Made in the USA
Columbia, SC
12 February 2023